A WALK IN THE PARK
Anthony Browne

Hamish Hamilton · *London*

Copyright © 1977 Anthony Browne
First published in Great Britain 1977 by
Hamish Hamilton Children's Books,
Garden House, 57–59 Long Acre,
London WC2E 9JZ
Reprinted 1980, 1982

By the same author

Through the Magic Mirror
Bear Hunt
Bear Goes to Town

Printed and bound in Great Britain by
William Clowes (Beccles) Limited
Beccles and London

One morning Mr. Smith and his little girl, Smudge, took their dog, Albert, for a walk.

On that same morning Mrs. Smythe and her so

...harles, were taking their dog, Victoria, for a walk.

Smudge, Mr. Smith, and Albert
went into the park.

Mrs. Smythe, Charles, and Victoria
arrived soon afterwards.

Albert was impatient to be let off his lead.

Victoria waited quietly until Mrs. Smythe had detached the lead from her collar.

Both dogs were free

They chased each other all over the park.

Mr. Smith went to sit at one end of a bench,
and Smudge sat with him.

Mrs. Smythe sat at the other end with Charles.
Smudge and Charles looked at each other.

Albert and Victoria raced along the
paths, dodging round trees, leaping
over flower beds. First Albert chased
Victoria, then Victoria chased
Albert, then Albert chased Victoria
again, so quickly that sometimes it
was difficult to tell them apart.

While the dogs played, Smudge and
Charles edged nearer and nearer
to each other.

Mr. Smith and Mrs. Smythe looked the other way.

Smudge went on the swings, swinging
higher and higher, as high as she dared.
Charles was not so sure.

Meanwhile an angry gardener chased the dogs off the flower beds.

They took off their coats and
Smudge swung like a monkey
on the climbing frame.

Albert felt too hot, so to cool himself he plunged into the fountain.

Smudge and Charles climbed a tree.

They all played on the bandstand.

The whole world seemed happy.

But Mr. Smith read his newspaper
at one end of the bench and
Mrs. Smythe looked the other way.

Charles picked a flower and gave it to Smudge.

"'Ere Albert, 'ere Smudge," yelled Mr. Smith.
"Time for 'ome!"

"Come here Victoria, come along Charles,"
called Mrs. Smythe. "Time for lunch."

Mrs. Smythe took Charles and Victoria home.

Mr. Smith took home Smudge and Albert.

And Smudge kept the flower.